Disney's

THE LITTLE MERMAID

THE DOLPHINS OF CORAL COVE

Disney's

THE LITTLE MERMAID

THE DOLPHINS OF CORAL COVE

by K. S. Rodriguez

DISNEY PRESS

NEW YORK

Look for all the books in this series:

Drawings by Philo Barnhart
Cover painting by Fred Marvin
Inking by Russell Spina, Jr.

Library of Congress Catalog Card Number: 94-70052

ISBN: 0-7868-4001-3

FIRST EDITION

1 3 5 7 9 10 8 6 4 2

For Ronnie Rodriguez and John and
Catherine Squires, with love

Disney's

THE LITTLE MERMAID

THE DOLPHINS OF CORAL COVE

"Tails up—one, two. Tails down—one, two . . ."

Deep beneath the ocean, six mermaid princesses—Alana, Andrina, Attina, Adella, Arista, and Ariel—swam gracefully in a circle under the direction of their oldest sister, Aquata. They were rehearsing the water ballet they would be performing for their father, King Triton, at his coronation day party, a yearly event celebrating the first day of his reign as King of the Sea. The party was less than a week away—but so far the rehearsal wasn't going very well. It was a beautiful day under the sea, and all the sisters were feeling a little distracted. Ariel found herself wishing more than once that she could be out swimming around and enjoying the day rather than stuck here rehearsing.

Still, she did her best to follow Aquata's instructions. "Now flip!" Aquata called out impatiently. "I said *flip!*"

The sisters flipped immediately after their cue, but then Andrina lost her balance and accidentally bumped into Aquata, sending her tumbling to the ocean floor.

"*Mmph!* Help!" Aquata shrieked. She struggled to untangle herself from some sea plants.

Her sisters tried to stifle their giggles as they rushed over to help her. Andrina was the only one who wasn't smiling at Aquata's predicament. "Sorry, Aquata," she muttered, her eyes downcast.

"That's it!" Aquata exclaimed, shaking a last bit of sea grass loose from her hair. "I can't do this anymore. Not one of you is paying attention or taking this seriously. I refuse to be embarrassed at Father's coronation party!"

The others glanced at one another in guilty silence.

"We're sorry, Aquata," Ariel said finally. "Please don't quit. You're the best choreographer we have."

"I'm the *only* choreographer you have. Besides, why should I bother? You're all totally distracted. Especially you, Andrina. What's gotten into you? You've never been this uncoordinated—you're usually the best dancer of all of us. But today you're pathetic! Now how can I possibly go on with everyone like this?"

Adella shrugged. "Aquata, maybe there's a reason why we're not paying attention," she said. "The ballet hardly seems worth paying attention to. I mean, it's just like the one we performed for Father last year. And the year before. And the year before that. Maybe we're . . . well . . . bored."

The other sisters gasped in surprise at Adella's bluntness. They looked at Aquata to see how she would react.

Aquata sighed and twirled a piece of her long brown hair around a finger. "As much as I hate to admit it," she said at last, "I think you may be right. I just can't seem to come up with anything fresh and new this year—it's not exciting to me anymore. I guess that's rubbed off on the rest of you."

While the sisters mumbled in agreement, Ariel noticed that Andrina was sulking off by herself instead of joining in the conversation. Ariel quickly swam over to her sad-looking sister.

"What's the matter, Andrina?" Ariel asked softly. When her sister didn't respond, Ariel put a hand on her shoulder. "We're all a little off today. Don't be upset—it's OK."

Andrina pulled away. "I'm fine! I just wish everyone would leave me alone and mind their own business," she snapped, then stormed away toward the palace. Ariel stared after her in surprise. Normally Andrina was cheerful and easygoing—not moody and bad-tempered, as she was today.

"Maybe I was a little hard on Andrina," Aquata said thoughtfully.

"Don't blame yourself," Alana told her. "She's been like this all afternoon."

"Alana's right," Attina agreed. "Andrina's sense of humor seems to have completely disappeared today."

"Not to mention her social skills," Adella added.

"I think we should let her be," Arista said. "She's probably just in a bad mood."

"Why don't we all take a break?" Ariel suggested.

Aquata shrugged. "We might as well," she said. "We're not getting anything accomplished here. We'll try again tomorrow morning."

"Well, then I'm going sea horse riding," Arista said. "Anyone else want to come?"

"I'll go with you," Adella decided.

"Me, too," Attina said. The three sisters went racing off toward the royal stables.

"I saw some beautiful new fish by the coral reef the other day," Alana said excitedly. "I've been dying to go back. Would you like to come?" She glanced hopefully at Ariel and Aquata.

"Sure, that sounds great," Ariel said.

"I was just going to sit here and try to think of new ideas for the ballet," Aquata replied glumly. "But that seems pretty hopeless. I guess I'll come with you, too."

"Great," said Alana. "Let's go!" She darted off in the direction of the coral reef, with Ariel and Aquata right behind her.

Ariel's long red hair flowed behind her as she glided through the sparkling water beside her sisters. They passed a family of wild sea horses grazing on some kelp. Then they saw some eels slithering in and out through the seaweed in a lively game of hide-and-seek. It seemed that every creature in the sea was enjoying the calm, clear day.

As they swam on, the sisters giggled and chattered. Even Aquata had managed to shrug off her worries about the ballet.

"Hey, Ariel, where's Flounder?" Aquata asked. "I thought he was planning to watch our rehearsal."

"He was," Ariel said. She wrinkled her nose. "But then Old Pike heard a rumor that humans were at Aqua Shore, and he made all the young fish attend a special emergency school session. You know how nervous he gets."

Alana shuddered. "Humans at Aqua Shore? Old Pike has a reason to be nervous, if you ask me. That's too close for comfort."

Aqua Shore was a cove located some distance beyond the coral reef. None of the merpeople in the kingdom had actually seen it, though—King Triton had passed a law forbidding any merperson from surfacing. Still, this was the first time the princesses had heard of humans being seen anywhere so close to the palace.

"Well, anyway, it means that poor Flounder has to sit through more lessons about how to recognize a baited hook," Ariel continued, shaking her head. "He wasn't hatched yesterday. He already knows these things!"

Aquata shrugged as she swam. "I don't understand what humans would be doing at Aqua Shore."

"Well, I heard that humans capture sea creatures and feed them to pet sharks," Alana said fearfully. "Or else they lock them up and make them their slaves for life!"

"That's not true!" Ariel said angrily.

"How would you know?" Aquata asked.

Ariel became quiet immediately. She didn't share her father's and sisters' mistrust of humans. She was fascinated by the world above the sea. In fact, she spent most of her free time searching for things that had fallen from ships. She kept her collection of human objects in a secret grotto near the palace. But Ariel had never told anyone but Flounder about her collection—she knew her father would be furious if he ever found out about it. He would be even more furious if he knew that Ariel sometimes surfaced to talk to her friend Scuttle the sea gull.

The last time Ariel had seen Scuttle, he'd told her about the humans at Aqua Shore. He said they were building some kind of wall right into the water. Ariel couldn't help but be curious about what the humans were up to.

"Let's race the rest of the way to the reef," Aquata suggested with a gleam in her eye. Her sisters accepted the challenge. Moments later the race was over and Aquata had won. Then the three sisters began exploring the colorful reef. Ariel was always dazzled by the array of beautiful fish that lived there. They came in all shapes, sizes, and colors. There were bottle fish, angelfish, sea cucumbers, spiny urchins, and many more. The mermaid sisters swam around the top part of the reef, enjoying the colorful sight of the abundant sea life all around them.

After a few minutes Ariel felt a small loach tug at her tail. The tiger-striped fish pointed at the ocean floor.

Ariel looked and saw an odd churning, way down at the bottom of the reef. "Hey, you guys," she called to her sisters. "Look at that."

Alana swam over. "What's going on?" she asked.

Aquata joined them as well. When she spotted the disturbance, she began to look worried. "What do you suppose is kicking up all that sand?" she asked.

Ariel shrugged. "Let's find out." She started swimming toward the churning, sandy cloud below them.

"Wait!" Aquata exclaimed. "Do you think it's safe?"

"There's only one way to find out," Ariel

called over her shoulder. Aquata and Alana exchanged a nervous glance, then shrugged and followed their younger sister.

As the sisters swam closer they could see that a large tail was thrashing at the water, causing the disturbance.

Alana gulped. "It may be a shark! We'd better turn around."

"Calm down," Ariel said. "It's only a dolphin. And it looks like she's in trouble."

The others looked more closely and saw that Ariel was right. The dolphin was nudging the reef with her nose. As the sisters rushed to her side, the dolphin turned to them with a look of distress.

"Help!" the dolphin cried. "My baby is stuck in the reef, and I can't get him out. If he doesn't surface for some air soon, he'll die. You've just got to help me! *Please!*"

Ariel, Alana, and Aquata immediately saw that the baby dolphin was wedged in a small space in the coral, with seaweed tangled around his fins. He let out small squeaks of fear as he struggled to free himself. The mermaids hurried to the young creature's side.

"Don't worry, we'll get you out," Ariel said soothingly. She and her sisters gently unwound the seaweed and carefully pulled the baby dolphin out of the crack in the reef.

"Oh, thank you! Thank you!" the mother dolphin cried. She wrapped her baby in her fins and rushed to the surface.

The mermaids were amazed at how fast the dolphin swam. Ariel looked up in awe as the mother dolphin broke through the surface.

A few minutes later the mother and baby dolphin returned. "Thank you all again," the mother dolphin said. "I couldn't get him out myself. At times like this I wish I had hands instead of fins!"

"We're glad we could help. I'm Aquata, and these are my sisters Alana and Ariel."

The mother extended a fin. "I'm Dolphine, and this is my baby, Phindolo."

"Thank you," the baby squeaked.

"How did you get stuck?" Ariel asked.

Phindolo seemed embarrassed. "I was trying to get a closer look at that funny-looking human object." Phindolo indicated something that was lying in the coral. Ariel rushed over to see.

"What in the world is it?" Alana asked. "Don't get too close, Ariel!"

"Don't be silly, Alana," Ariel said distractedly. She regarded the object closely. Its flat metal head, about the size of Ariel's face, was shaped sort of like a scallop shell, and it had a long, skinny wooden handle. It looked almost like the racket Andrina used when she played sandball.

"I told Phindolo that he should stay away from what he doesn't know. 'Curiosity killed the catfish,' you know. He doesn't listen very well," Dolphine said.

"We're always telling Ariel the same thing," Aquata said. "And she doesn't listen very well, either." She turned to Ariel, who was still gazing at the human object. "Now get your nose out of that coral before *you* get stuck!"

Ariel obeyed her sister—for the moment— and moved away from the reef. What a fine addition that object would be to my collection! she thought. She silently vowed to return for the object and bring it to her grotto.

"Why don't you come to Coral Cove with

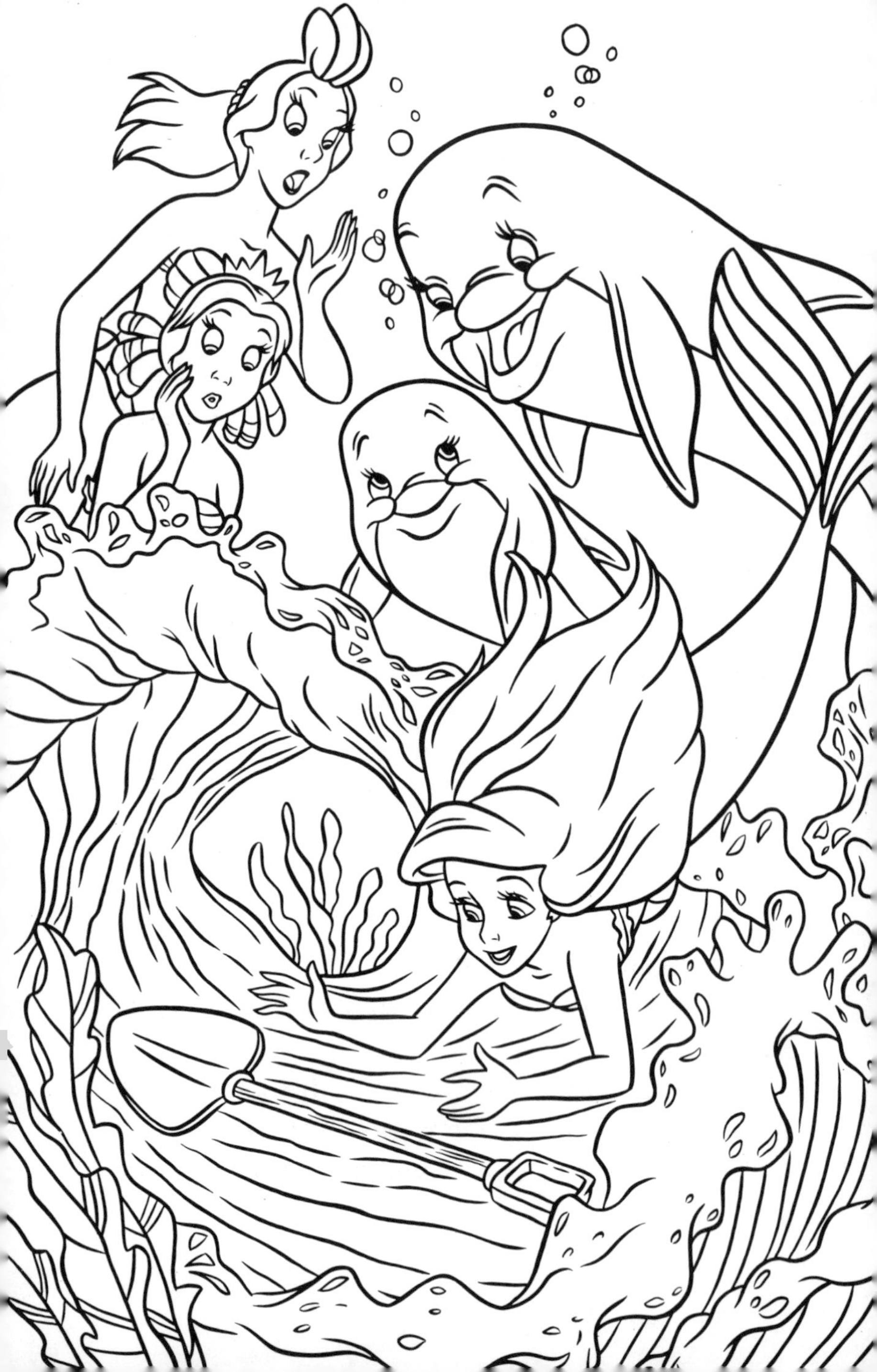

us?" Dolphine asked. "I would love to introduce you to the others. I know they'll want to meet the girls who saved my baby!"

The mermaids exchanged glances. "Thank you. We'd love to come," Aquata said. Alana and Ariel nodded in agreement.

As she and her sisters followed Dolphine and Phindolo to Coral Cove, Ariel looked up toward the surface wistfully. She couldn't stop thinking about how wonderful it must be to be a dolphin. She imagined surfacing whenever she wanted, maybe even meeting some humans. . . . She sighed deeply and hurried to catch up with the others.

The mermaids could hear the squeals of frolicking dolphins as they approached Coral Cove. "This is awfully close to Aqua Shore," Aquata whispered to her sisters, sounding a little nervous.

Dolphine called out, and soon two other dolphins swooped over to greet them.

"I'm Madolpha," one said, doing a graceful back flip.

"I'm Marino," the other dolphin said, a broad smile on his bottle-nosed face.

"Not one of you overgrown minnows

finished your plankton stew!" a plump squid scolded loudly, waving a ladle as she bustled out of the cove. "And you two missed lunch," she added to Dolphine and Phindolo. Abruptly she noticed the three mermaids. "Oh, you didn't tell me we had guests! My name's Samantha. But you can call me Sammy." She extended three tentacles, one for each sister to shake.

"Where's Rudolph?" Marino asked.

"He's finishing your leftover stew, as usual," Sammy informed him. "If he keeps eating this way, he'll have to join a whale pod soon!"

"Hey, aren't you King Triton's daughters?" Madolpha asked suddenly, staring at the mermaids.

The princesses nodded. Dolphine gasped. "Oh my goodness! I didn't even recognize you! I hope you'll forgive me—I guess I was just too worried about Phindolo to think straight."

"What happened?" Sammy demanded.

Dolphine quickly told the others about how the mermaids had rescued Phindolo.

"They were so clever," she finished with a sigh.

Sammy sighed, too, letting out a stream of bubbles. "Honestly, I don't know what I'm going to do with these flipper-brained creatures," she exclaimed to the sisters. "I don't know how many times I have to tell them to keep away from humans! All they do is lead you into trouble or feed you too many snacks before dinner."

Another dolphin tumbled out of the cove. "Did someone say something about snacks?"

Ariel, Alana, and Aquata giggled. "You must be Rudolph," Alana said.

"Right you are," the chubby dolphin replied. "Now, did I hear something about human treats?"

"Not so fast, whale boy!" Sammy snapped. "You've had enough to eat for today. Besides, I was just saying that I think you should end *all* contact with humans. They're nothing but trouble!"

"But the humans think we're cute," Madolpha said. "They'd never harm us!"

Rudolph and Marino nodded in agreement.

17

"I'm beginning to agree with Sammy," Dolphine said slowly. "If Phindolo wasn't so interested in humans, he would never have gotten stuck."

Phindolo put his head down, and his tail drooped. "Don't be ashamed," Ariel whispered to him. "I understand how you feel." Phindolo brightened at Ariel's words and nuzzled against her.

"I used to work in a dolphin pod where they were all captured by humans—the whole bunch of them," Sammy said, fluttering her tentacles dramatically. "Now I hear from some of my sea gull friends that they're being forced to perform tricks for the humans' amusement. What kind of life is that?"

"We agree with you," Aquata said. "Humans are trouble. Everybody knows it."

Sammy nodded. "Anyway, can I offer you girls some plankton stew—or what's left of it?"

Before the mermaids could answer, Rudolph interrupted. "I finished all the stew," he said sheepishly. "Even what was in the pot."

Sammy shook her tentacles in frustration. "But we have *guests*!"

"That's OK," Alana said, looking a little relieved. "We've already had lunch." She winked at her sisters. Plankton stew was definitely *not* their favorite dish.

"Well, at least we can try to make up for it by showing you a good time." Sammy turned to the dolphins. "Why don't you entertain our guests while I clean up."

"Gladly," Rudolph said.

Marino wiggled his fins in excitement. "Let's play!"

The mermaids each grabbed a dolphin's fin as they darted off.

Ariel chuckled as she held on to Rudolph. "Wow, you guys are fast!" she called breathlessly. She glanced back and saw that Aquata and Alana were right behind her, holding on to Marino and Madolpha. Dolphine and Phindolo zoomed alongside.

The dolphins glided joyfully through the water, doing somersaults and loop-the-loops.

"Oh, this is fun!" Alana cried.

They swam up, down, over rocks, under

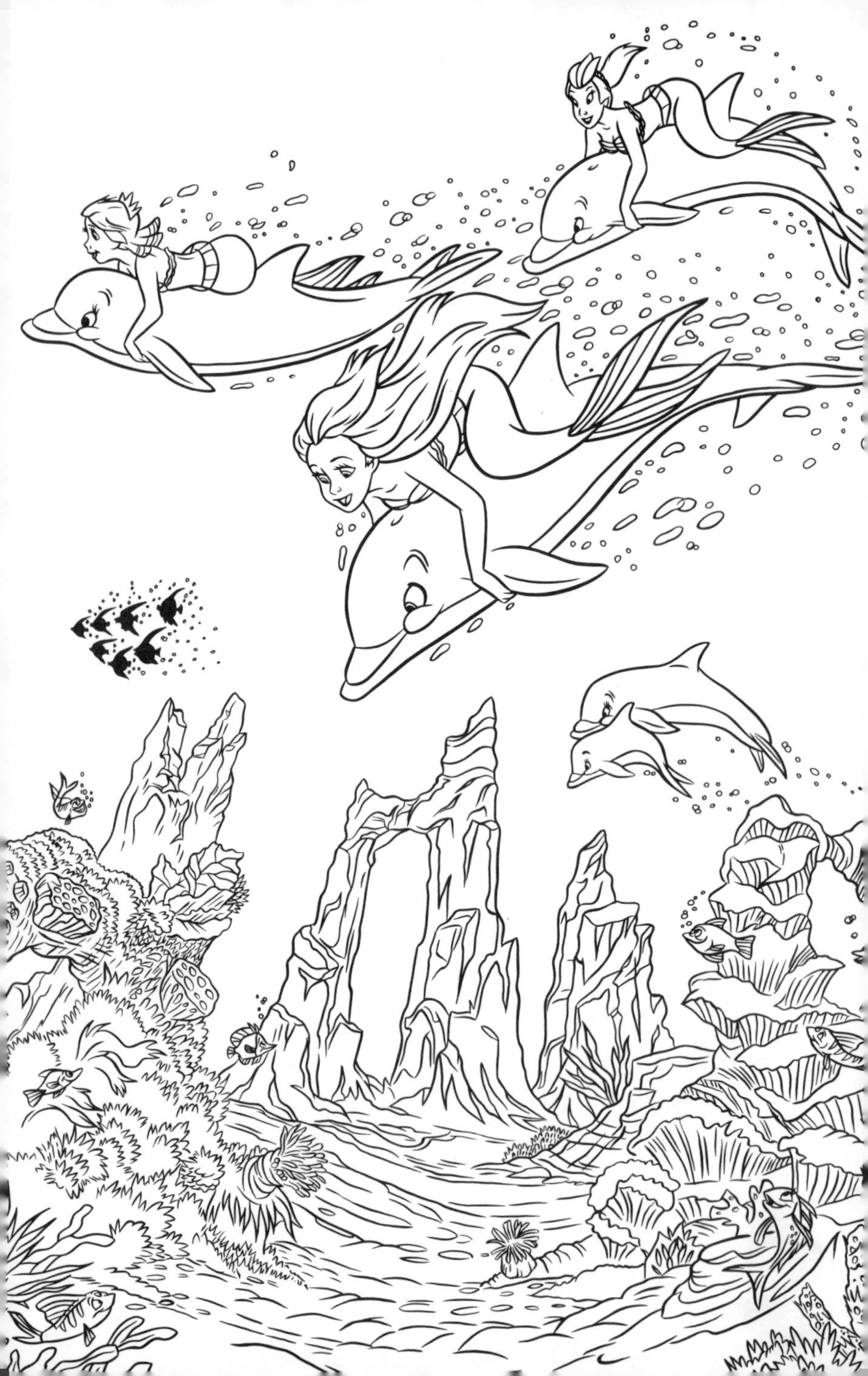

coral archways, and sideways through sea grass. Ariel was amazed by the way the dolphins did triple flips and twists so effortlessly. She marveled at their gracefulness and poise. Suddenly she gasped and asked Rudolph to stop. "Aquata! Alana! I just had the most wonderful idea!"

Her sisters let go of Marino and Madolpha and swam over. They were smiling, and their faces were glowing. Ariel could tell they were having as much fun as she was. "What is it, Ariel?" Alana asked, her eyes still on the dolphins, who had started chasing one another in and out of a nearby cave, squealing gleefully.

"Let's ask the dolphins to be in our ballet!" Ariel exclaimed. "They'd be wonderful!"

Aquata's eyes lit up. "Ariel, that's perfect! They're just what we need to make the ballet special."

"They could leap up in the center of our circle and do a triple turn coming down—," Alana began.

"And we could ride them while they do somersaults," Ariel added.

"I can't wait to start choreographing it," Aquata said.

"First we'd better ask them if they want to do it," Alana pointed out.

Ariel nodded and called the dolphins over.

"What's happening?" Dolphine asked with concern. "Why did you stop? Were we going too fast?"

"No, nothing like that," Aquata assured them. "Ariel just had the best idea. Tell them, Ariel."

Ariel crossed her fingers, hoping the dolphins would agree to her plan. "Would you like to be in our water ballet? We'll be performing it for our father's coronation day celebration next week."

"We don't have much time to rehearse," Aquata added. "We'd all have to work hard. But it would be fun, I promise!"

"Oh, that sounds wonderful!" Madolpha cried. "I've always wanted to be a star."

"It does sound like a lot of fun," Dolphine said. "Count me in."

"I think we're all in agreement," Rudolph said, looking over at Marino and Phindolo, who nodded eagerly. "It would be an honor to perform for King Triton."

"Great!" Ariel exclaimed.

"Are you sure you'll be around for the next few days?" Alana asked. "I know sometimes dolphins travel pretty far."

"Definitely," Dolphine assured her. "Phindolo is still too young to go long distances. We'll be here."

Aquata smiled and clapped. "Then it's all set! We'll hold our first rehearsal tomorrow morning at the palace. I hope you don't mind practicing on a Saturday."

The dolphins shook their heads.

"We can introduce you to our other sisters then," Alana said. She looked at Aquata and Ariel. "I can't wait to tell them about this. Come on, it's almost time for dinner. We'd better head back."

"How about one more ride before we go?" Ariel suggested.

"I don't think so, Ariel," Aquata warned. "We have a long swim back to the palace."

Ariel frowned. "Then you two go ahead. I'm not going to be a worry-clam. I'll be home in time. I'm just going to stay for one more short ride."

Aquata rolled her eyes. "OK, have it your way. But don't expect me to cover for you if you're late and Father gets angry."

"Don't worry. I won't be late. See you later," Ariel said as she grabbed on to Rudolph and sped away. Her sisters waved and swam off toward the palace, still chattering excitedly about the ballet.

Ariel laughed gleefully, soaking up the freedom she felt as Rudolph whizzed through the water. Rays of sunlight from the surface reflected off the rocks and sea plants in arcs of aqua and emerald. The soft dark sand on the ocean floor glittered with bits of mother-of-pearl. Everything is just perfect, Ariel thought. It's a beautiful day, I've made some new friends—and soon Daddy's water ballet will be perfect, too!

Ariel held on tight. Rudolph dove down and skimmed along the ocean floor, so close that Ariel's hand could graze the sand. Then he made a quick turn and raced upward, higher and higher and faster and faster. The water got brighter and bluer as they neared the surface. Suddenly they broke through and emerged into the air as Rudolph leaped into a high arc.

"How wonderful!" Ariel gasped as she sped through the white foam of the waves.

During the seconds they seemed to hang suspended in the air, Ariel felt the warm afternoon sunlight on her shoulders. Drops of water were clinging to her long eyelashes. She squinted, and the golden afternoon sun and bright blue sky became a rainbow of colors.

When Rudolph sliced back into the water, Ariel felt the rush of the sea welcoming her back.

"Do it again!" Ariel cried.

"Hold on!" Rudolph answered.

This time Rudolph leaped even higher. Ariel laughed with exhilaration. "I feel like I'm flying!"

The dolphins gathered around and took turns lifting Ariel high in the open air above the waves. Ariel had never had so much fun in her whole life.

Sometime later as Ariel broke through the water holding tight to Marino's fin, she noticed that the sky was turning pink and violet. The sun was setting! She had lost all track of time.

"I'm going to be late for dinner," Ariel

cried when they were back underwater. "My father will be so angry!"

"Your father!" Dolphine gasped. "Ariel, you're not supposed to surface! I can't believe we forgot that and broke King Triton's law. Please forgive us!"

"It's not anyone's fault but mine," Ariel said. "It's easy for you to forget. You're allowed to surface."

"I'll give you a ride," Madolpha offered. "I'll have you home in a flash—you forget how fast we are."

Ariel smiled in relief. She knew that the dolphin could take her home much faster than she could swim herself. But she still felt a little guilty about surfacing. Her father's law seemed so silly—but silly or not, she decided, it was the law, and she really should obey it. She vowed not to do any more surfacing.

"Good-bye!" Ariel called to the other dolphins as she and Madolpha raced off. "I'll see you tomorrow. Thank you for everything. And please thank Sammy for me, too!"

Madolpha swam faster than ever. Ariel realized that Coral Cove was farther from the palace than she had thought. As they neared the reef, Ariel remembered the human object. She felt a little guilty about asking Madolpha to stop, but she figured that since she had vowed not to surface anymore, at least she should be able to keep her collection. After all, there was no law about that.

Ariel retrieved the object and was surprised at how heavy it was. Madolpha helped her carry it. "It looks kind of like a big heavy fish skeleton without the ribs," Madolpha observed. "What do you call this?"

"I don't know," Ariel answered. She wished she could ask Scuttle. He almost always knew the names of Ariel's human treasures. But if she couldn't surface, she couldn't talk to Scuttle. Ariel sighed. Being an obedient daughter sure was difficult!

In what seemed like no time, they reached Ariel's secret grotto. Ariel moved the rock that blocked the entrance, and she and Madolpha swam inside.

Madolpha looked around the huge, bright cavern in awe. "Wow! This is incredible."

Steep, high walls of white sea rock loomed on either side of them. The cave was filled with all kinds of curious objects.

"Quite an impressive collection you have here," Madolpha said.

"Don't forget, this place is a secret," Ariel reminded her.

"I promise not to tell a soul. But let's go now, before you're *really* late."

After Madolpha dropped her off, Ariel raced through the courtyard into the palace. She arrived at the dinner table just as everyone else was sitting down. King Triton didn't seem to notice Ariel's slight tardiness. But Sebastian, the crab who was the king's chief adviser and the princesses' music teacher, glared at Ariel crossly. She gave him a dazzling smile. Sebastian sighed and rolled his eyes. "Princesses!" he muttered under his breath.

As the cook brought out the first course, King Triton cleared his throat. "Daughters, I have something to talk to you about. There have been some human sightings at Aqua Shore." The King stroked his long white beard thoughtfully. "As long as you all stay well underwater, you should be fine. As I always say, the sea takes care of its own. But I'd really prefer that you try to avoid the whole area near Aqua Shore for a while—just until we know what the humans are up to."

Ariel played with her food and tried to shake her guilty conscience. She realized that her father made these rules because he really cared about his kingdom—and especially about his daughters. She knew he didn't want any harm to come to them.

Ariel sighed. She felt sorry for her father, who seemed preoccupied with the troubles of the sea. After a whole day of disobeying him, Ariel decided that she would give her father a secret present. From now on, she resolved, I will be the best daughter possible!

Ariel smiled, and ate with gusto. Playing with the dolphins had made her hungry. "Pass the sea salt, please," she asked Andrina.

Andrina listlessly passed the shaker to Ariel. Ariel noticed that Andrina hadn't touched her food. "Why aren't you eating?" she asked.

Andrina didn't answer.

"Yeah, that's odd," Adella chided, her mouth full of food. "Something *must* be wrong if Andrina's not eating."

"Don't speak with your mouth full, Adella," the King said. He turned to Andrina. "What's wrong?" he asked gently.

"I'm not hungry," Andrina responded quietly.

"Are you ill?" the King pressed.

"Maybe. May I be excused?"

The King nodded. "Get some rest, my dear."

Without another word, Andrina rose from the table and slowly floated away.

The six remaining sisters looked at one another with concern. They were all thinking the same thing: This was not the Andrina they knew. What in the world was wrong with her?

The next morning the mermaid sisters waited anxiously for the dolphins to arrive. Ariel, Alana, and Aquata had told the other sisters about Ariel's idea after dinner the night before. They all thought it was a wonderful plan—and that it would be a magnificent surprise for King Triton. Even Andrina had seemed to brighten a little bit.

Sebastian and Flounder were there, too. They had offered to give the mermaids some pointers from the audience's perspective.

Now all they needed to begin were the dolphins.

As the sisters waited, a group of merboys swam past carrying shells, driftwood bats, and other seaball equipment. Andrina frowned when she saw them.

One boy spotted her and waved. "Hey, Andrina!" he shouted with a grin. "We've been looking for you. Are you going to join us in a game later on?"

"No, Neptony," she said coldly. "I won't be playing with you guys today. Good-bye."

Neptony seemed hurt. "But . . . we need our star pitcher!"

"What do we need her for, anyway?" another merboy said rudely. "Let's go!"

The merboys started to swim away. But Neptony hung back for a moment, staring at Andrina with a puzzled look on his face.

"Bye," he finally said, and swam off after his friends.

"When have you ever refused a game of seaball?" Arista asked.

"I don't feel like playing today. Plus, we've got the ballet to finish," Andrina replied. "Where are those dumb dolphins, anyway?"

"They *are* kind of late," Aquata said. "I hope they remembered."

"Well, dolphins tend to be a little flighty," Attina pointed out.

"But they were so excited yesterday," Alana said. "I'm sure they'll be here soon."

"You know, I'd really like to watch your rehearsal," Sebastian said. "I'm sure I could give you girls some pointers. But I don't have all day."

Ariel gave her sisters a worried look. "Something must be wrong. They probably got mixed up about the time we were supposed to meet. I'd better swim over and find out."

"Wait just a second, young lady," Sebastian said. "Coral Cove is awfully close to Aqua Shore. Weren't you listening to your father last night when he asked you to try to stay away from there?"

"But what if something has happened to the dolphins?" Ariel pleaded. "Please, Sebastian, you have to let me go. I'll take Flounder with me."

Flounder seemed startled, but he agreed. "Don't worry, Sebastian. We'll be careful."

"Besides," Ariel pointed out, "Daddy didn't

exactly say we *couldn't* go near Aqua Shore. He just said it would be better not to. Please say I can go, Sebastian! Pretty please?"

Sebastian frowned. He glanced from Ariel to Flounder to the other princesses, then back to Ariel again. She gave him a hopeful smile. "Oh, all right," Sebastian relented grumpily. "But you must promise me you'll be careful—and that you'll turn back at the first sign of trouble."

Ariel nodded. "I promise."

"All right then." Sebastian turned and headed for the palace. "Honestly," he grumbled to himself. "The things I have to put up with around here . . ." His voice trailed off. The princesses giggled.

"Come on, Flounder," Ariel said. "Let's go." As they swam off, Ariel whispered, "On the way back maybe we'll stop at the grotto for a minute. I've got an interesting new object to show you."

"Don't be too long," Aquata called after them. "We're going to start rehearsing without you."

Flounder and Ariel sped off toward Coral Cove. Sebastian's warnings echoed through

Ariel's mind. She thought that Flounder seemed a little nervous, but she figured that was because Old Pike had been scaring him again.

But as they paddled on, Ariel couldn't help but notice that something seemed different about the sea today. It was darker than yesterday, and a strange eeriness in the water made Ariel feel a little uncomfortable.

"How far is this place, anyway?" Flounder asked breathlessly a few minutes later. "I'm getting tired."

"We're almost there," Ariel assured him.

When they finally reached the entrance to Coral Cove, Ariel knew something was wrong. She remembered hearing the squeals of delight from the rambunctious dolphins yesterday as she approached. Today the cove was completely quiet. There was not a ripple in the water, and no one came out to greet her and Flounder.

"Hello!" Ariel called. She waited, but no one answered. "Hello!" she shouted again, louder. There was still no response.

"I—I don't like this place," Flounder said fearfully. "Let's go."

"Not until we find out what's going on," Ariel said, beginning to feel a little frightened herself. What could have happened to the dolphins?

"Hello!" she called once again. When there was still no answer, Ariel decided to go in. Flounder reluctantly followed.

"Maybe they moved on," he suggested.

"I don't think so," Ariel said. "Just yesterday Dolphine said that Phindolo couldn't travel very far."

Inside, the cove was completely deserted. Ariel and Flounder swam around looking for clues.

"Wait a minute," Ariel exclaimed as she examined a conch shell half-full of plankton stew. "They didn't finish their breakfast!"

"So?" Flounder asked.

"So, Rudolph *always* finishes off the leftovers. And besides, Sammy Squid would never leave such a mess," Ariel explained, her voice full of worry. "It's as if they just dropped everything and left in a hurry. Something terrible must have happened." But she couldn't imagine what.

As they swam out of the cove, Ariel and Flounder questioned every sea creature they could find. They talked to lobsters and mussels. They stopped a herd of zebra fish. They asked crabs, abalones, and clams. But no one had noticed anything.

"Phindolo! Dolphine!" Ariel cried in frustration. "Madolpha! Rudolph! Marino! Sammy!"

"Madolpha! Rudolph! Marino! Sammy!" Flounder repeated hopefully.

There was no answer. The sea was oddly silent.

"I guess we should go back to the palace," Flounder suggested. "Maybe they left word there. Maybe your sisters have found out something."

"Not yet, Flounder. There's someone we've forgotten to ask," Ariel said. She turned and sped away, her face full of determination.

"Wait up!" Flounder called after her.

As they swam, Flounder realized where they were going. They were headed toward the small island where Scuttle the sea gull lived. "Oh no, Ariel! We promised Sebastian we'd be careful!"

"We *will* be careful," Ariel said. She tried not to think too much about what she was planning to do. She was about to break not only one of her father's strictest laws but her personal vow as well. Still, she had to find out where the dolphins had rushed off to in such a hurry. After all, her father did always say that the sea takes care of its own. How could he be angry at her for trying to help fellow sea dwellers?

"Ariel! Please stay underwater," Flounder begged.

Ariel ignored her friend and cautiously peeked out of the water. Nothing but a bit of red hair and a pair of bright blue eyes showed above the surface.

"Hey, is that you, Ariel?" Scuttle squawked. He flapped down and landed on a rock near the shore of the island. "What's up, kiddo?"

"Oh, Scuttle, the dolphins are—"

"Hey, sweetie, you're bubbling, not talking! How's about lifting your mouth outta the water?" Scuttle said.

Ariel slowly lifted her head and shoulders out of the ocean. Flounder bobbed to the surface and swam around her nervously.

"I promised myself I wouldn't surface anymore," Ariel told Scuttle. "You know— because of Daddy's law."

Scuttle peered around carefully. "Ain't no humans around here. It's OK to come on up."

Ariel pulled her body up onto the sand, much to Flounder's horror.

"A-A-Ariel—," he sputtered from the water.

The sun washed over her body, warming her with its golden rays. "It's OK, Flounder," Ariel said, tipping her face up to enjoy the feeling of the sunlight beaming down on her. "This is an emergency. I think even Daddy would understand, just this once."

"He wouldn't! I know he wouldn't!" Flounder called from the water. "Come back in, Ariel!"

"What kinda emergency?" Scuttle asked curiously. "What's cookin'?"

Ariel quickly told him about the dolphins. "I thought you might be able to spot them from the air. Will you help us, Scuttle, please?"

"Sure thing, kiddo. I was thinking about giving my wings a stretch anyway." He began to flap. "Stick around. Be back in a sec."

Ariel watched him take off and soar into the sky. Soon he was just a tiny black dot against the setting sun.

At Flounder's urging, Ariel slipped back into the water. But she kept her head above the surface, looking out for Scuttle. Finally,

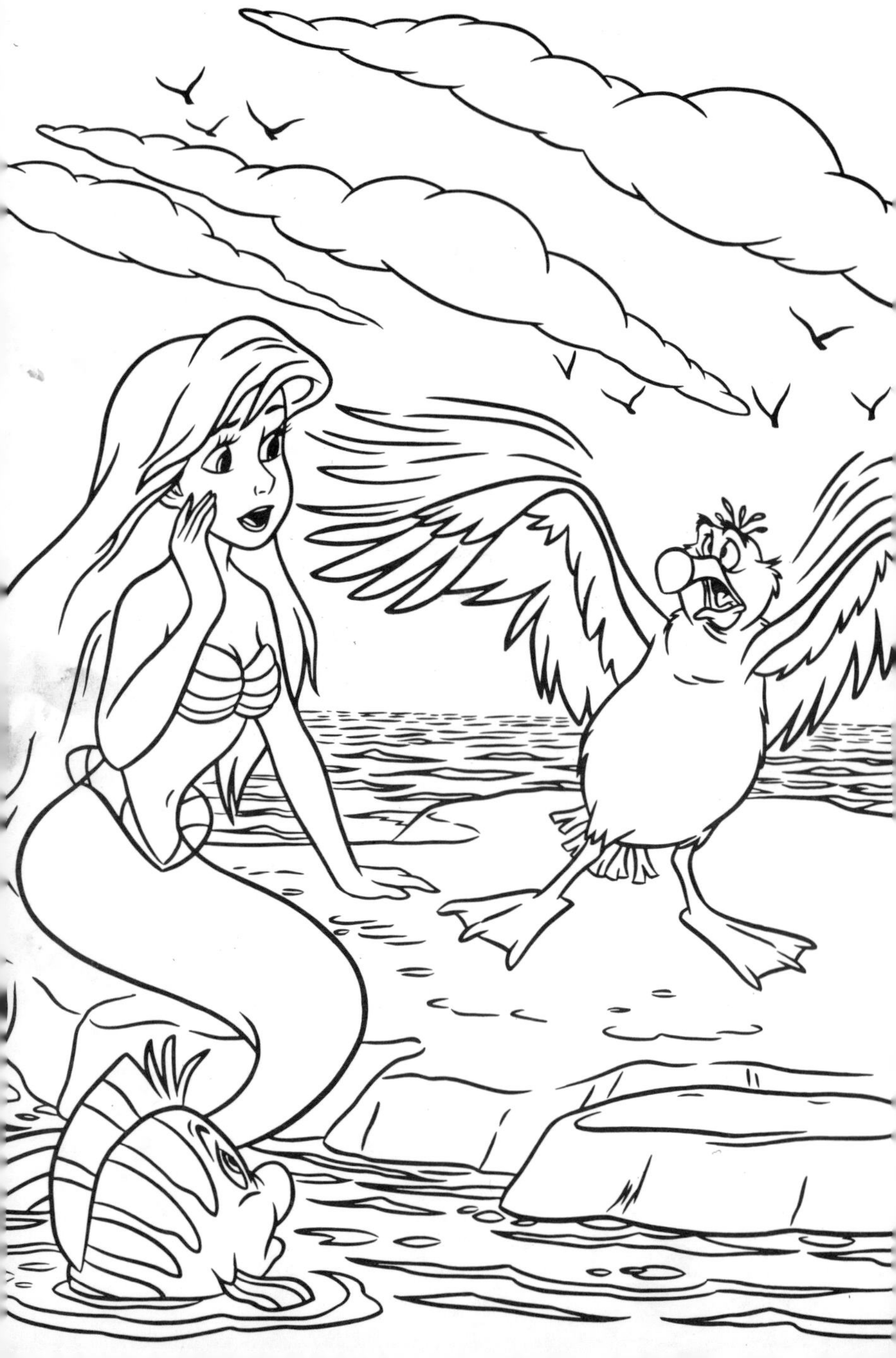

after what seemed like an eternity to the anxious mermaid, Scuttle swooped down and landed on the same rock.

Ariel quickly pulled herself out of the water again. "Did you see the dolphins?"

"Sure did. All the way over at Aqua Shore."

"Aqua Shore! What are they doing there?" Ariel wondered anxiously.

"Search me." Scuttle scratched his feathers. "Remember I told you about that weird wall the humans were building? Well, there's a big commotion going on in the water nearby. A lot of splashing and stuff. So I swoop down low and see four dolphins swimming in circles just outside the water wall, kicking up a mess of foam."

"Four dolphins? But there should be five," Ariel said.

"Four dolphins—that's what I saw. They're hard to miss, those fellows."

"You didn't see a little one?" Ariel asked anxiously.

"Can't say that I did. But you know what they say. Size is relative."

"What does that mean?" Ariel asked.

"I have no idea," Scuttle replied. "It's just what they say."

"Well, thanks a million, Scuttle," Ariel said. "You've been a big help."

"Anytime, sweetie. Come back soon, you hear?"

Ariel dove back into the water. "Come on, Flounder. We're going to Aqua Shore!"

6

Ariel swam as fast as she could toward Aqua Shore. Flounder trailed behind, trying desperately to keep up.

"I just hope we don't get in trouble," Flounder moaned.

"We're doing the right thing," Ariel reminded him. "The dolphins are in trouble, and we have a responsibility to help." Ariel swam faster than ever. Flounder groaned and followed. The pair startled many sea creatures as they sped past in a blur.

One sea creature was particularly surprised. Samantha Squid waved her many arms to flag down Ariel and Flounder.

Ariel recognized her immediately. "Sammy!"

"Ariel! Please help! We're over at—"

"I know, Aqua Shore. What's happening?"

"Phindolo's been trapped by the humans," Sammy explained. "I was just on my way to get help, but I can't move as fast as I used to."

"We're on our way," Ariel said, ready to swim off.

"But wait! How did you know we were at Aqua Shore?" Sammy asked, confused.

Ariel hesitated. She was afraid Sammy might be upset if she knew that Ariel had surfaced. "Just a good guess. See you back there!" She zoomed off, with Flounder beside her. Sammy struggled along behind them. After a few seconds they had left her far behind.

When Ariel arrived at Aqua Shore, the dolphins were relieved to see her. Dolphine, Madolpha, Rudolph, and Marino rushed over and, talking all at once, explained the situation.

"There was a ship above Coral Cove this morning—"

"We were having breakfast but decided to swim up to see—"

"Sammy had gone off for her morning swim—"

"She always warned us—"

"Phindolo swam toward the ship—"

"They had treats—"

"He got too close—"

"They had a net—"

"He's trapped in this pen!"

Ariel held her hands up and spoke soothingly. "OK, OK. I'm here to help," she assured them. She swam over to examine the pen. So this was the wall that Scuttle had told her about. What in the world was it for? Maybe Alana was right—maybe humans used this pen to trap sea creatures and feed them to pet sharks! Maybe all the other terrible things Ariel had heard all her life were true, too! The possibilities reeled through Ariel's mind. She had always been so sure that humans were kind and wonderful—but what if she were wrong?

The square wooden pen stretched out from the beach to enclose a section of ocean about the size of Ariel's secret grotto. The high walls were covered with a net to prevent Phindolo from jumping out.

"There's a door," Dolphine told Ariel. "We can't open it with our fins, and Sammy wasn't strong enough to budge it. But maybe you can get it open."

Ariel and Flounder swam to the door in the side wall.

"Thank goodness the door's underwater," Flounder said. "We can try it without the humans' noticing."

"They've been gone for a while," Rudolph said. "We wouldn't be making so much noise if they were here. We've been watching out for them—we just hope they don't come back soon."

"Be careful, Ariel," Flounder whispered.

Ariel approached the door. She pulled on the handle while Flounder peeked through the keyhole.

"I see him!" Flounder exclaimed.

They could hear Phindolo's whimper through the door.

Ariel tried to comfort the baby dolphin. "Hold on. We'll get you out," she said soothingly.

Although Ariel pulled on the door with all her might, it just wouldn't move. "It's locked tight," she said to Flounder.

Phindolo whimpered again. "Don't worry. I'll think of something else," Ariel said, trying to sound convincing.

Ariel swam back and forth, surveying the pen from every angle. Flounder hovered anxiously nearby with the dolphins.

Sammy arrived, panting and wheezing, and approached Ariel nervously. "Any luck? We can't get him out, can we?" Before Ariel could answer, Sammy threw up her tentacles in despair. "I knew it! I knew something like this would happen if they spent too much time around humans. But do those silly dolphins listen to a word I say? No! Why, I might as well be talking to myself. . . ."

But Ariel wasn't listening to the distraught squid. "I won't give up!" she muttered to herself while still gazing at the pen. "Now let's just think. If Phindolo can't come through the walls, and he can't get over them . . . maybe, just maybe, he can come *under* them! That's it!"

Sammy stopped swimming frantically back and forth and stared at Ariel in excitement. "You mean you think we can dig him out from under?"

"Exactly," Ariel said.

Sammy fluttered her tentacles. "Then let's get started!"

Sammy, the dolphins, and Flounder dove to examine the bottom of the pen. The walls seemed to be sunk deep in the ocean floor, but the door had only a few inches of sand piled up against it. By shoving her hand down into the sand, Ariel could just feel the bottom edge of the door.

"I see," Rudolph said. "We can dig in the sand below the door and make a hole big enough for Phindolo to swim through! Brilliant!"

" 'We' means Ariel and me, flipper-face," Sammy said. "You can't dig with your fins."

"Sorry," Rudolph said glumly.

Ariel and Sammy grabbed some shells and

started to dig. They dug as fast as they could, but after a few minutes they had barely made a dent in the shifting sands.

"This will take hours," Sammy said. "We'll never be able to make a decent hole. These shells just aren't big enough."

Ariel knew Sammy was right. If only I could find a bigger shell, she thought. She stared down at the small shell in her hand and wondered where she would be able to find a bigger one. Ariel tried to imagine a bigger shell shaped like the one she had. It made an elongated half-oval—almost like a fish head.

The answer came to Ariel, plain as day. The human object would be perfect to dig with!

Ariel called Madolpha over and explained her plan. "We'll be back shortly," she told the others. "Keep watch for humans."

"But where are you going?" Sammy asked in a panic. "We've got to keep digging! Those fish-eating, pen-building humans could come back any time now."

"It's our little secret," Madolpha said, smiling at Ariel. "But don't worry. We'll be back soon to get Phindolo out."

"Hurry!" Dolphine called after them.

Ariel took hold of Madolpha's fin, and they whooshed off.

Moments later they arrived at Ariel's secret grotto. Ariel lingered outside for a second, glancing around to see if the coast was clear. Just then she heard a familiar, nervous voice.

"Oh, Ariel, there you are! Where in the world have you been? And who are you, my dear dolphin friend? Why have you been keeping Ariel? What are you two up to?"

"Sebastian!" Ariel cried. Her heart sank. She didn't know what to do.

Sebastian stood on a rock and peered straight into Ariel's eyes. "What's the matter, girl?"

"Oh, nothing. Absolutely nothing. You just startled me. Sebastian, this is my friend Madolpha."

Madolpha gave Sebastian a wide smile.

"Charmed, I'm sure," Sebastian said. "Your sisters want to know what's going on. They've almost finished their rehearsal."

"I can explain, sir," Madolpha said politely. "One of us is ill, and Ariel has been nice enough to help out. We just came back to let everyone know that we're OK and that we'll be by to rehearse soon."

Sebastian regarded Madolpha and Ariel suspiciously.

Ariel tugged at Madolpha's fin. "So, Sebastian dear, could you please let everyone know that we'll be back soon? I just wanted to bring some fresh kelp to little baby Phindolo to make him feel better. If you could pass on our message, I'll be able to help Phindolo sooner."

"Well . . . OK," Sebastian agreed reluctantly. "But hurry—and I hope you're being careful!"

"We are! See you later."

Ariel and Madolpha pretended to leave but instead swam in a circle.

"That was a close call," Ariel said when they came back to the grotto. They quickly moved the rock that blocked the entrance. "Thanks for covering for me. Sebastian means well, but if he knew what I was doing, he'd have a fit! And my father would never understand."

Madolpha smiled. "It's OK. Don't forget, the sea takes care of its own."

Ariel hugged Madolpha, then quickly

located the human object. She grabbed hold of Madolpha's fin once more, and the dolphin swam out of the grotto at top speed.

Sammy, Flounder, and the others were waiting anxiously when Ariel and Madolpha arrived back at Aqua Shore.

"Why, it's that troublemaking human object," Dolphine said in amazement when she saw what Ariel was carrying. "The one that Phindolo was looking at yesterday when he got stuck!"

Ariel nodded. "Now it's going to help him get free," she said. "It'll help us dig. Watch!" She dove to the bottom and stuck the flat metal part of the object into the sand. Grasping the handle, she pulled a big chunk of sand away from the door and dumped it behind her. As Ariel continued to dig and dig, she uncovered the bottom part of the wooden door, and a hole started to form underneath it. Then the current started working for them rather than against them, washing more sand out of the hole. Ariel continued to dig furiously. With help from Sammy's tentacles—each one holding a shell— the hole grew bigger and bigger.

"Phindolo!" Ariel gasped at last. "Can you fit through yet?"

Phindolo swam over and peeked through the hole hopefully. But Ariel could see right away that he wouldn't be able to fit.

"Hold on," she called. She and Sammy continued to dig. Although Sammy's tentacles flew as fast as ever, the squid was panting with exhaustion. Ariel's arms were so tired she could hardly feel them as she scooped more sand out of the hole. Still, she knew that without the human object they would never have been able to dig so fast.

"I think it's big enough now," Sammy gasped at last, collapsing on the sand.

Ariel looked through the hole at Phindolo, who was watching anxiously. "OK, try now," she said. She moved back to give him room.

The baby dolphin propelled himself toward the door, held his breath, and squeezed into the hole. He writhed and wiggled, trying to work his way through.

"Uh-oh, I think he's stuck," Flounder whispered.

But Phindolo wasn't giving up. He closed his eyes and wiggled even harder, a

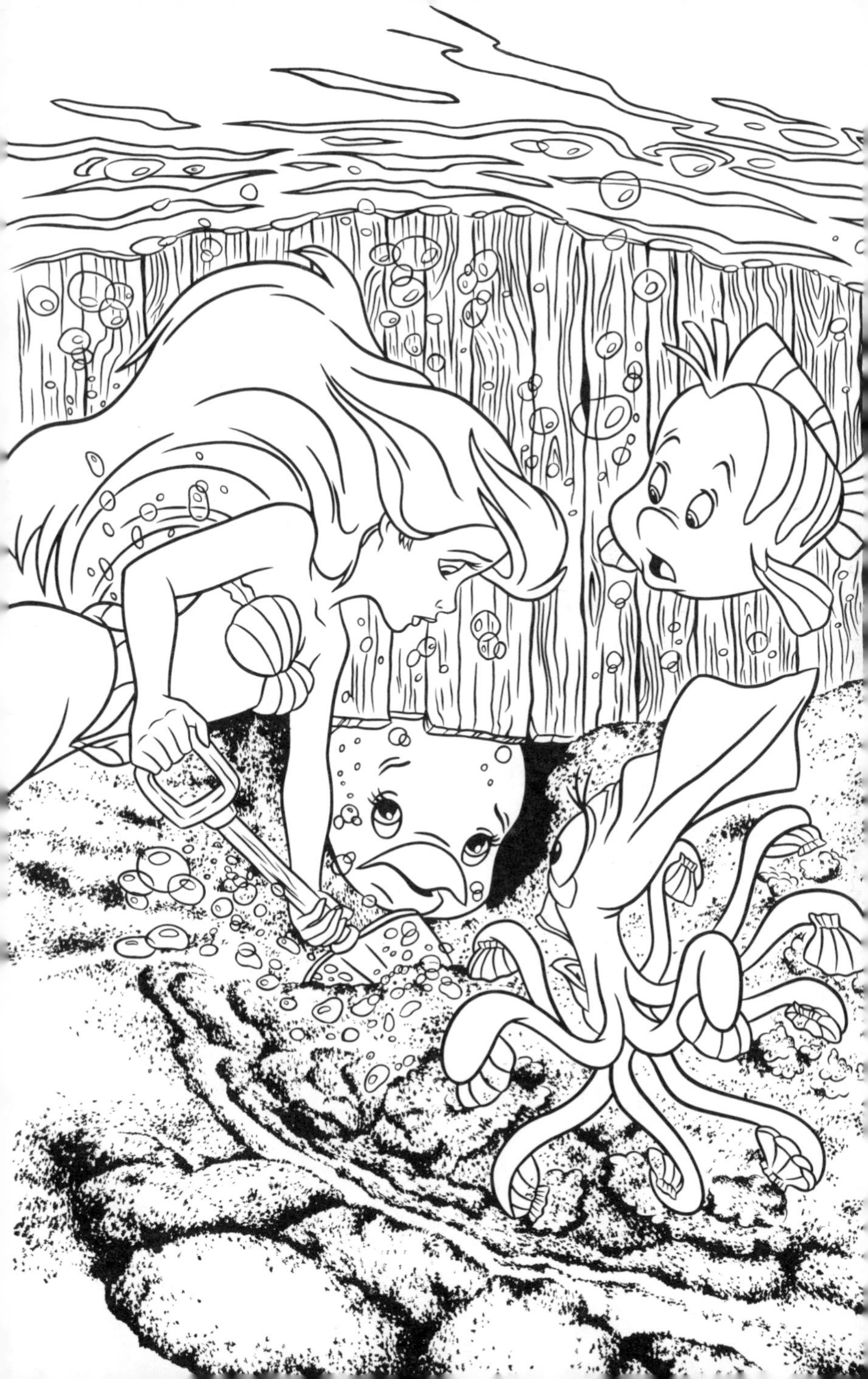

determined look on his face. Ariel crossed her fingers. Finally, with a whoosh of water and sand, Phindolo popped through. He was free! The other dolphins let out squeals of joy. Dolphine rushed forward to hug her baby. Ariel and Flounder exchanged smiles.

Just then a large shadow darkened the ocean. A ship was moving toward them overhead.

"I hate to break this up," Sammy said, "but we'd better get out of here before you coral-brains get us into more trouble."

"All right, Sammy," said Marino meekly. "From now on I think we're all going to pay more attention to your advice. Right, gang?"

The other dolphins nodded. Then they all headed back to Coral Cove. Madolpha clapped her fins. "Now let's celebrate," she exclaimed. "I think Ariel deserves a party, don't you?"

"Definitely," Dolphine agreed.

Phindolo swam over and nudged Ariel with his little bottle nose. "Thanks for rescuing me—again," he said.

She hugged him and smiled. "You're welcome."

"Come on, let's get this party started," cried Sammy, wiggling her tentacles. "To Ariel!"

"To Ariel!" the dolphins chorused.

For the next half hour they frolicked, played, laughed, and danced. Ariel had never had so much fun. Then, suddenly, her festive mood changed.

"Oh no," she gasped, bringing her hand to her mouth. "My sisters! They're waiting for us to rehearse! I told Sebastian we'd be back soon. I've been gone for hours! They must have the search school out for me. What do I tell them?"

Sammy Squid put a tentacle around Ariel's shoulder. "Don't you worry. We'll tell them exactly what happened. You'll be a hero."

Ariel's eyes grew wide. "But you can't—if they know that I was surfacing, I'll be in big trouble!"

"Surfacing?" Sammy repeated. "But technically you didn't surface. You were near the surface, but you were really underwater the whole time."

Ariel gulped. "Well, not exactly," she admitted. If she was going to ask Sammy and the dolphins to keep her secret, she figured she'd better be completely honest with them. "You see, I found out where you were by surfacing and talking to my sea gull friend, Scuttle."

Sammy's eyes widened. "Scuttle?" she exclaimed with delight. "You know Scuttle?"

"Why, yes," Ariel replied, surprised at the reaction. "Do you know him, too?"

Sammy laughed. "You bet I do! That old birdbrain and I go way back! I'll have to pay him a visit soon. How is he doing these days? I can't believe you know old Scuttle!"

"He's fine," Ariel replied. "But anyway, Daddy must never know that I talk to Scuttle. He'd never forgive me!"

"Well, why didn't you say so in the first place!" Sammy said. "I've been known to tell a white lie or two—especially for a hero."

"Thank you!" Ariel looked around at the dolphins hopefully. "Are we all agreed?"

"All I know is that you saved my baby's life again—of course, while totally submerged in water—and nowhere near any humans," Dolphine said, laughing.

Ariel was so excited that she did a flip.

"OK then. Time to dance. Back to the palace, everyone!"

When Ariel, Flounder, Sammy, and the dolphins arrived at the palace they were greeted by Sebastian and six worried mermaid sisters. They immediately began bombarding Ariel with questions.

"Where have you been?" Aquata asked.

"We've been waiting," Adella said pointedly.

Arista crossed her arms over her chest. "What took you so long?"

"Are you OK?" Attina asked.

But Sebastian drowned them all out. "Do you have any idea what time it is, young lady?" he bellowed. "I thought you said you'd only be gone a few more minutes!"

"And that was hours ago," Aquata added. She shook her head. "At least it gave me plenty of time to work out all the choreography for the ballet."

"Yeah," Adella said grumpily. "And she made us practice it about a zillion times."

Alana changed the subject then by introducing the dolphins and Sammy to Attina, Adella, Arista, and Andrina. The first three sisters greeted them warmly, and

Andrina gave a halfhearted little wave. Ariel could see that her mood hadn't improved any since the day before.

When the introductions were finished, Sebastian cleared his throat sternly. "All right now, Ariel," he said. "We're still waiting to hear where you've been all this time."

Then Sammy spoke up. "Please, dear sir, allow me to explain," she began, with a secret wink at Ariel.

The seven mermaid sisters gathered in the hallway outside the royal concert hall, whispering and giggling with excitement. Their father's coronation day celebration was in full swing. Octavio, the one-octopus band, was getting ready to take the stage. When his performance was finished, it would be the princesses' turn. They had worked hard all weekend perfecting their water ballet, and there was no doubt in their mind that it would be their most spectacular performance yet. They helped one another straighten their shimmering multicolored costumes one last time.

"I hope those dolphins aren't going to be late again," Adella commented.

Just then the dolphins came swimming in breathlessly. They spotted the princesses and hurried over. They were each wearing a different colored bow tie that matched the colors in the mermaids' costumes.

"There you are," Aquata said. "We were just starting to worry."

"Sorry about that," Rudolph said, straightening his tie. "We lost track of time."

Sammy waved her tentacles in frustration. "So what else is new?" she complained. She was dressed in a colorful flowing gown that made her look like a beautiful ocean flower. "I *try* to keep them on schedule. But it's just too big a job for one squid to handle!"

Ariel laughed. "You did fine, Sammy."

"Yeah," Phindolo piped up. "We're here, aren't we?"

The mermaids all laughed, even Andrina. Ariel was glad to see that the festive mood of the grand celebration had chased away her sister's moodiness. The palace was glittering in the moonlight sifting down through the water. There was a special magic in the air, and all of them felt it.

Madolpha went to the door and peeked into the concert hall. "My, there's quite an audience out there," she commented. It was true. Guests had come from far and wide to attend the party. There were dukes, duchesses, earls, counts, and barons from all the seven seas. Countess Oystera was sitting in the second row with her husband, Count Halfshell. The mermaids had already seen most of their friends from school. It seemed that everyone in the kingdom—and beyond—had come to wish King Triton well. The King himself was seated in the middle of the front row, and his daughters could tell he was having a wonderful time.

The princesses, the dolphins, and Sammy crowded around the door and listened as Sebastian introduced Octavio, who began to play a selection of the King's favorite songs. As he launched into *Concerto in Sea Minor* by Mozshark, the sisters were distracted by the sound of someone calling Andrina's name. They turned to see Neptony, the merboy from her class, hurrying over.

Instantly Andrina's happy mood vanished and her frown returned. "Hello, Neptony," she said coldly.

He stopped in front of her, wide-eyed. "Andrina, you look—you look beautiful!" he exclaimed.

She blushed and turned away from him to hide her embarrassment. Adella was glancing from Andrina to Neptony and back again, a knowing smile on her face. She grabbed Andrina by the shoulders and spun her around to face the merboy. Andrina shot her a dirty look, then glared at Neptony. "What do you want, Neptony?" she asked curtly.

"I just want to talk to you for a second," he said quietly. "To apologize." He cleared his throat, and his voice got louder. "I know I acted like a jerk at school on Friday, and I'm sorry. Some of the other guys were making fun of me for hanging around you so much, and I was trying to prove I didn't like you." He took her hand and gazed into her eyes. "But the truth is, I *do* like you,

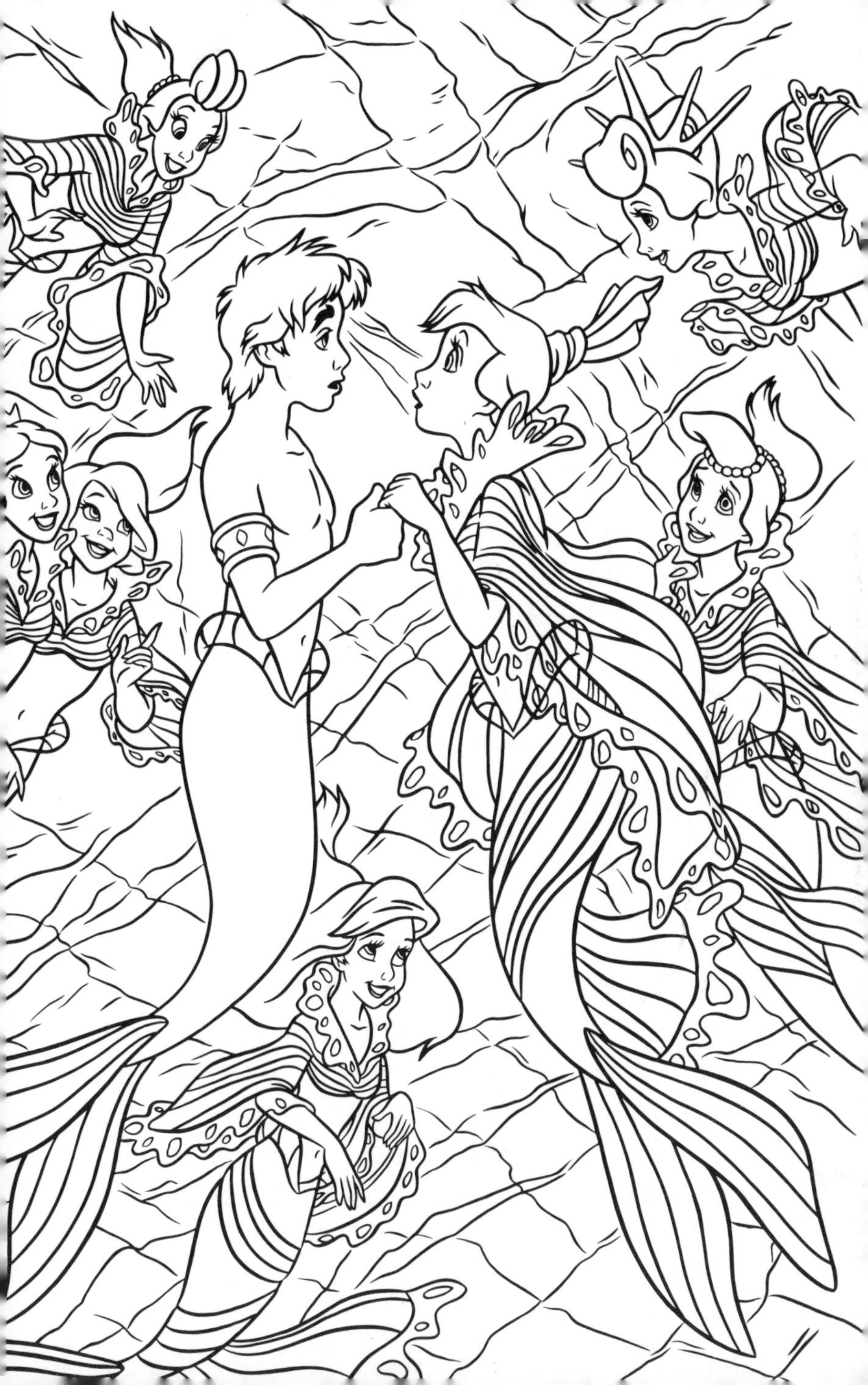

Andrina. And I don't care who knows it."

Andrina's expression softened. "Really?" she whispered.

"Really." He nodded. "My friends are just jealous because they're too immature to talk to girls. But *I'm* not—not anymore." He cleared his throat again, looking nervous. "In fact, I was wondering—would you go out with me next weekend? Maybe we could play a little finball, then go out for a soda or something. . . . If you'd like to, that is."

Andrina smiled. "I'd love to," she replied.

They stared at each other for a few more seconds, not quite sure what to say.

"Ahem," Adella said. "I hate to break this up, but we'd better get backstage. We have to go on in a few minutes."

"Oh!" Andrina glanced around at her sisters, who had been listening eagerly to every word, and blushed again. Then she turned back to Neptony. "Maybe I'll see you after our performance," she said shyly.

He grinned. "That would be great. Good luck with the ballet, Andrina. Oh, and the rest of you, too." He hurried off toward the door into the concert hall, still smiling.

As soon as he was gone, Andrina's sisters turned to her expectantly.

"Well?" Adella demanded. "Would you care to explain what that was all about?"

"Yes, Andrina," Attina added, a little more gently. "Why didn't you tell us about Neptony?"

Andrina shrugged. "I was too embarrassed," she admitted. "Most of you have boyfriends already, and I wasn't sure you'd understand. I really liked him, and I was pretty sure he liked me, too, but then he started ignoring me and even making fun of me in front of his friends." She shuddered. "I mean, I can take a joke as well as the next person—"

"Or better," Ariel broke in. The others laughed. Andrina was well known for her sense of humor.

Andrina laughed, too. "But somehow it wasn't so funny this time, you know?"

Arista nodded understandingly. "You could have talked to us about it, though," she told Andrina. "After all, some of us have had problems with our boyfriends, too. Remember how afraid I was that Father wouldn't approve of Dylan?" Dylan was a stableboy who worked at the summer palace. He and Arista were crazy about each other.

"And then there was that mix-up between me and Tedrick," Attina added with a sidelong glance at Adella. Not long ago Adella's matchmaking had almost ruined things for Attina and the boy she liked. Luckily, things had turned out all right in the end, and Attina and Tedrick had been dating ever since. "And Aquata has had a few arguments with Nexar, remember?"

Alana nodded. "And don't forget, not all of us have boyfriends," she told Andrina, glancing at Ariel and Adella.

"Speak for yoursef, Alana," Adella said frostily. The sisters laughed. Adella didn't have a steady boyfriend—but she always seemed to have more boys hanging around her than she could count.

Andrina smiled at her sisters. "Thanks, you guys," she said gratefully. "Next time I have a problem I'll talk to you about it. I promise."

"Well, I don't think you'll be having any problems with Neptony anytime soon," Attina said slyly. "He seemed *very* sorry."

"Not to mention *very* cute," Adella added.

Andrina blushed. "Anyway, I'm sorry I was so grouchy all weekend," she said, obviously trying to change the subject.

"It's OK," Ariel said. "Love makes you do the craziest things."

Just then the dolphins and Sammy came swimming over. "The octopus just finished," Sammy reported.

Aquata gasped. "Uh-oh! We'd better get backstage—pronto!" She darted for the backstage door with her sisters, the dolphins, and Sammy right behind her.

The ballet was a smashing success. The audience was spellbound by the marvelous choreography and awed by the dolphins' acrobatic moves. When the performance was over, the crowd applauded wildly. Ariel noticed her father's proud, beaming face as he clapped harder than anyone.

When the sisters came off the stage, their father swam over to them. "Thank you, Daughters!" he boomed, sweeping them all up in his arms for a group hug. "That was marvelous! Absolutely marvelous!"

"Thanks, Father," Aquata said. "But we

did have some help, you know." She gestured to the dolphins and Sammy, who were hovering nearby.

"Of course," King Triton said, turning to them with a smile. "A wonderful job, all of you."

"It was an honor to perform for you, Your Majesty," Dolphine replied for all of them. She gave a little bow.

King Triton nodded. "Well, it's an honor for me to have such talented subjects," he said. He hugged the princesses again. "Not to mention such talented daughters. You girls never cease to amaze me."

"They're pretty amazing, all right, Your Majesty," Sammy said with a secret glance at Ariel. "More amazing than you know!"